Belle

Christmas on Dewberry Lane

Book Four

Cheryl Wright

Copyright

Belle

(Christmas on Dewberry Lane Book Four)

Copyright ©2021 by Cheryl Wright

Cover Artist: Black Widow Books

Editing: Amber Downey

Dedication

To Margaret Tanner, my very dear friend and fellow author, for her enduring encouragement and friendship.

To Alan, my husband of over forty-six years, who has been a relentless supporter of my writing and dreams for many years.

To Virginia McKevitt, cover artist and friend, who always creates the most amazing covers for my books.

To You, my wonderful readers, who encourage me to continue writing these stories. It is such a joy knowing so many of you enjoy reading my stories as much as I love writing them for you.

Table of Contents

Chapter One

Dewberry, Montana – 1880s

Belle Armstrong stood at the counter of her candy store and glanced about.

She could do this, she knew she could. With Christmas nearly upon them, she had to prepare for the weeks ahead. It was always a busy time of year for Belle; apart from the additional work she had making enough candies for her eager customers, loneliness always hit her this time of year.

Not that she wanted to marry – that was the last thing on her mind. But having someone to share the happy times with, as well as a friendly ear to listen to her worries, would make her life a little easier. Several of her friends had recently married, and it left her feeling as though there was a void in her life.

Belle shook herself – she did not need a man in her life to be happy.

The bell over the door tinkled, and she brought her mind back to the present. "Good morning, Mrs. Grayson!" Belle was genuinely happy to see her elderly customer.

Ethel Grayson brushed the snow from her thick coat and pulled off her expensive gloves. "Good morning, my dear." She glanced at the young woman, giving her the once-over. "Is that a new apron you're wearing?"

Belle smiled. "It is. I thought I would splurge for Christmas. What do you think?"

The older woman reached out and fingered the embroidery along the top edge. "It's quite beautiful. You surely had it hand-made? I doubt you could find anything like that in Dewberry." She stared at Belle pointedly, waiting for an answer.

"As a matter of fact," Belle said quietly, as though someone might hear them, "I got it from *Buttons and Bows*. Ivy put it aside when it arrived and gave me first option."

"How wonderful!"

It really was wonderful, and Belle was grateful to her friend Ivy for her thoughtful gesture. "Is there something specific you're after today, Mrs. Grayson?" She could stand and chat all day, and this customer would gladly do so, but Belle simply didn't have the time. She still had a batch of boiled sweets to prepare. The jars should arrive in the next day or two, and she dearly wanted the sweets to be ready for packing by then.

"Honestly, I don't know. I have a craving for something sweet. Any suggestions?"

Mrs. Grayson visited the Candies Galore store at least once a week. The widow was lonely, and frequented all the stores on the Dewberry Lane shopping strip. No one minded because she was a selfless person who supported those who needed it.

Every year when the Christmas tree went up on Dewberry Lane, it was Mrs. Grayson who ensured the charity box was filled with toys and other wonderful goodies. Belle sighed. They needed far more people like Mrs. Grayson in Dewberry. She glanced down into the glass cabinet.

"What about some fudge?" She pulled out a tray, offering a sample to the woman standing opposite. "They are quite delicious, if I do say so myself." She winked at her customer. "I made these only last night. You couldn't get them any fresher."

Mrs. Grayson closed her eyes and Belle watched as contentment passed over her face. "My dear girl! They are more than delicious – this is by far the best fudge I have ever tasted."

Warmth filled Belle at the kind words passing Mrs. Grayson lips. Whether they were truth was another thing altogether. "I would like four boxes please."

"But…" Belle floundered a little. "They don't come in boxes." She glanced about the store. She had boxes for some of her other candies. "I could use these boxes if that suited your purpose." She extracted four pretty blue boxes from a cupboard behind her. They were reserved for the special candies she made only at Christmas. They were not overly large, and each had a big gold bow on top; perfect for the holiday season. "Are they for gifts?" Belle was curious more than anything.

"Very likely." Mrs. Grayson didn't commit herself more than that. Everyone in Dewberry knew about Ethel Grayson's charitable escapades. The woman spent up big in town, but rarely kept anything for herself. If someone was in need, she would hone in on them, and ensure they never went without, especially if there were children concerned. "Add it to my account, and I will settle up today."

Belle packaged up the purchases and placed them in a brown paper bag. "Thank you Mrs. Grayson," she said, handing over the bag. The woman paid up her account, then opened the door to leave.

"Who is that out there?" she suddenly demanded.

Belle stretched her neck trying to see, but Mrs. Grayson's carriage blocked her view. She came around to the other side of the counter. "I have no idea who that is. A salesman perhaps?"

Her hand waving in the air, the older woman seemed quite displeased. "I don't like strangers. You know that Belle."

Everyone knew that, but Belle wasn't sure what she was supposed to do about it. Not knowing what else do to, she held the door open for her customer. The man in question seemed to be wandering about Dewberry Lane, then suddenly went into the Holly-Berry Cake Shoppe, seemingly having found the place he was looking for. Belle closed the door as Mrs. Grayson was handed into her carriage and went back behind the counter. It was nearly time for closing. She had been at the store far too long and was looking forward to taking a break.

Busy tidying up the cupboard where she'd taken the boxes from, Belle spun around as the door opened again. "Did you forget something Mrs. Gray…" The words froze on her lips when a good looking man stood before her. "Oh." Oh indeed. She recognized the man from earlier – he was the stranger Mrs. Grayson had pointed out. Like her customer, Belle did not like strangers; she was more comfortable with people she knew.

He thrust a hand in front of her. "Caleb Bligh. Very happy to meet you Miss…?"

Belle looked him up and down. The man before her was confident despite being a complete unknown in this town. Too confident if you asked her – who knew what the man was up to. He pulled his hand away when she didn't reciprocate, hurt written all over his face.

"Armstrong," she finally replied. "Belle Armstrong. What can I do for you, Mr. Bligh?" She didn't like salesman. Most of those she dealt with tried to strong-arm her into buying their wares. There wasn't much Belle required for her store, apart from consumable food products, and quickly rid herself of them. "There is nothing I need to purchase at this time." It was the mantra she recited time and again, keeping salesmen at bay.

Now he appeared disappointed. Then he stared at her chest. Belle's heart pounded; was this man some kind of sex fiend? She needed to get out of the store, and now. She was alone and if he cornered her, help would be beyond her.

"I see you already have one," he said, his eyes returning to her face.

Now she was confused. "Excuse me?"

"The apron. I came in here to sell you some of my aprons, but you are wearing one. Where did you get it?"

Warm air escaped from her mouth, and she fingered the hand embroidery on the apron she wore. "*Buttons and Bows.* Ivy sold it to me." She smiled now, more than a little relieved her first thoughts had left her mind.

He smiled, and it lit up his face. "Good." He floundered a little. "It…er, looks good on you." He reached into a satchel and pulled out a number of small packages. "I have more here; all with a different pattern. Some Christmas, some not." He pulled two out of their paper wrap. "I particularly like this one," he said as he held it up for her to see.

It was pretty, real pretty, and it was hard for Belle to resist. "I do like that," she said quietly. "How much are they?" Silly question she realized. Ivy sold the apron she wore at cost price. The price rolled off his tongue, and it matched what Ivy told her, so at least she knew he wasn't trying to cheat her. "Can you show me more designs please?" He held them up one by one, and Belle ended up buying five more. That way she had a clean apron for every day, although not all of them had a holiday design on them.

"I have other linens too. They're out on the wagon. Tablecloths, kitchen towels, sheets, bedding."

Belle shook her head. "I have no need for such items." She glanced about her little store. "As you can see, I have no tables here. No one buys candies and stays to eat them." She laughed, and he suddenly stared at her, as though he was seeing her for the first time.

Belle reached down and handed him a wad of money – payment for the aprons. "I would like a receipt please." She didn't really need one, but she liked to keep the books in order. Besides, she didn't know this man. How did she know he wouldn't turn around and say she hadn't paid him? It was better this way.

"Supper?" He stared at her, not moving from the spot where he'd stood through this conversation. The moment the words were said, he fiddled. It was as though he regretted the words the moment they were out of his mouth.

"Excuse me?" Belle studied him. She hadn't really seen him before, she was too busy trying to get rid of the man.

"I'm asking if you'd like to have supper with me. We both have to eat, and, well, I don't like eating alone." He busied himself with the remaining aprons as he spoke. "You'd think I'd be used to it by now."

Yes, you would. But he was right – Belle hated eating alone, but what could she do? That was her life; eating and living alone. Doing everything alone. Before she could stop herself, Belle was accepting the stranger's invitation. "It does sound lovely. I accept." She slipped the apron up over her head and hung in up on the hook she kept for precisely that reason.

"I noticed *Ma's Kitchen* up the road. I've already made a booking for two."

He'd made a booking for two? "But you hadn't asked me. We hadn't even met." Fury rose up inside her. Was she being played?

"I make a booking for two in every town I visit. In my experience, there's always someone who would enjoy my company. Or a free meal." He grinned, and if she hadn't been such a lady, Belle might just have slapped his egotistical face. "I don't mean…" He scowled. "I didn't mean to come across as arrogant. I have invited elderly ladies, and men, to dine with me." He winked then, as though that made it all right.

"Well, in that case then…" Belle knew her words sounded sarcastic, but she couldn't help herself. The man was trouble and was already getting under her skin.

"Good. Are you ready now, or should I pick you up somewhere later?"

Did he truly not understand her sarcasm, or had he chosen to ignore it? Either way, she was feeling rather irritated by this complete stranger. She should send him on his way, never to see his impertinent face again. Only she felt drawn to him, and it was annoying the heck out of her.

Feeling more flustered than she'd ever felt before, Belle reached for her warm coat and gloves, then ushered him out of the store. She locked the door behind them. "I am ready now," she said, having absolutely no idea why she had agreed to dine with this haughty man.

He offered her his arm, and Belle accepted his silent invitation. Warmth immediately enveloped her.

After returning the excess aprons to the wagon, they headed towards *Ma's Diner*. It was the only diner in town, Belle told him. She also said it was one of the only two eating establishments in Dewberry. The other one was the saloon, which accommodated a far lower class of customers.

Belle wouldn't walk near there, let alone dine there, even accompanied she'd said assertively. Was she sending him a message? That should there be a repeat performance, it better not be at the saloon? Caleb Bligh was amused at that thought and placed his hand over hers. It felt good having her so close, but there would be no repeat. He would be gone from Dewberry tomorrow, or the next day at the latest.

This was probably the smallest town he'd visited so far, and there were few stores that would be interested in his products. Of course he was unaware of that when he'd decided to go there, but it was on the way to his next stop, which was far larger. No matter, it was worth the time, and was no hardship.

If he was honest, he preferred small towns in some ways. He loved the friendships and friendliness he always encountered in the smaller towns. A man could get lost in places like Helena. Besides, it was far more difficult to find someone who wanted or needed some company.

If he was honest with himself, Caleb could easily settle in a town like Dewberry. The problem was, what would he do there? He was a traveling salesman, and his work involved moving from one place to another on an almost daily basis.

As they reached the diner, the door suddenly opened, and a young woman ushered them in out of the cold and the snow he hadn't even realized was falling until removing his coat. Was he so comfortable with the delightful Belle Armstrong that he'd become oblivious to everything around him? That simply wouldn't do. The sooner he got out of Dewberry the better.

"Good evening! Welcome back Mr. Bligh." He was surprised she remembered his name, but again, a small town trait. "Hello, Belle. Nice to see you."

The two women chatted away like old friends as Merry helped them out of their coats. She led them to a table by the window, but truth be told, Caleb would have preferred somewhere a little more secluded on this occasion. Belle was such a delightful companion, and he couldn't have asked for anyone better.

"The food here is wonderful," Belle told him as they read through the menu. "It won't matter what you order, it's all delicious."

"You know this from experience?"

"Of course. Her mother taught Merry everything there is to know about cooking. Sadly Ma is no longer with us, but her legacy lives on."

"Ah, *Ma's Diner*. Now it's beginning to make sense."

Merry returned shortly and took their orders, then left them alone again. It wasn't long until their food was placed in front of them. "You were right, the food here is delicious. If only I were staying long enough to sample the entire menu." He felt genuinely disappointed, and not only because of the food. The company he currently kept was quite appealing to Caleb as well. He couldn't recall another instance where he'd wished he could stay longer. Most of his dining companions had been elderly women, many of them store owners, like Belle, but none as enticing as her.

"Can you not? I mean, do you not set your own schedule?" She lifted her eyebrows and his heart thudded. Was this genteel woman asking him to stay longer? Caleb shook himself mentally. Of course she was right, but the longer he stayed, the harder it would be to leave. Besides, it would also mean a loss of income because whenever he didn't sell his wares, he didn't earn money. He couldn't do that for very long.

"I can, but if I linger too long, it would take far too long to visit all the towns. Then it would be more like a holiday." He grinned and his words made her laugh. Her dainty laugh was more like a tinkle, and he wanted to hear more of it.

Merry brought a mug of coffee for each of them, interrupting the pleasant conversation. Caleb couldn't recall a time he'd enjoyed supper so much. Not for a very long time anyway. There was a time, but he'd prefer to forget that tumultuous time in his life. It hadn't ended well. "Shall we order dessert?" Anything to distract his mind from those difficult times.

Merry handed them both the dessert menu. "These are tonight's desserts. Would you like me to wait, or shall I come back?"

Caleb glanced over the offerings. "Cherry Cobbler sounds good." He glanced across at Belle and she nodded. "Cherry Cobbler for two, thank you." While they waited, Caleb glanced out the window next to their table. "Looks like the snow is becoming quite heavy. Hopefully it slows down tomorrow."

"If you know Montana, you know to expect anything." Belle licked her lips, and a look of sadness overtook her. Did she feel the way he did? He'd never felt so connected to anyone, especially a woman, for many years.

"You're right of course, but a man can wish, can't he?" In this case, he was half wishing for the snow to continue at this heavy pace, but also wanted to leave. He couldn't afford to get attached to any woman, especially not one in a small town that he would rarely visit. It just wasn't right.

He shook the thought away as Merry delivered their dessert.

Once the meal was over, he would walk Belle home, and that would be the end of their affiliation. With that determination in mind, he concentrated on enjoying the remainder of the evening with his charming companion.

Chapter Two

The evening had been one of the most satisfying in a long time. The snow fall had kicked up and could almost be described as a snowstorm. But it wasn't quite there yet. Belle lived above the store, she'd reluctantly told him, and honestly, he couldn't blame her. A single woman living alone had to be cautious. He'd insisted as he needed to assure himself she got home safely. Dewberry might be a small town, but they would still have criminal types lurking around every corner.

There was no way he would allow himself to let her walk home alone in the dark, *and* in the snow. His conscious simply wouldn't allow it. Caleb reveled in the warmth of her arm on his, and he took the liberty of enclosing his hand over her much smaller one. The pity of it all was that if he'd been in a position to stay longer, he would jump at the chance. Belle Armstrong really appealed to him, even after such a short acquaintance. He had no idea why, but wouldn't question it.

He had often prayed to God to help him find his soulmate, and perhaps Belle could be that to him, but the timing was off. His next stop was the Bozeman Fair, where he could make a killing. Last time he went there, he sold out of every item in his wagon, and had to return to Helena to collect more stock. He was almost salivating just thinking about the money he would make. Not that money was important to him – Caleb spent his life traveling. There was little to spend money on except meals and accommodation.

As they reached Belle's apartment, for which the stairs were situated at the back of the store, the snow became far heavier. He was relieved to get her home in one piece. "I'll wait down here and watch you go inside," he said as she placed one foot on the bottom step.

She turned to him before going upstairs. "I had a wonderful evening. Thank you for inviting me." Was that sadness he saw in her eyes? "It's a pity you can't stay longer."

It was true. He could easily stay longer, but for both their sakes, he dare not. He would eventually have to leave, and that was the truth of the matter. "Unless this weather lets up, I'll be here an extra day. Otherwise, I'll leave tomorrow. I enjoyed our evening together and thank you for your company." He tugged at the brim of his hat, then waited for her to enter the apartment. Caleb watched as she entered, then waited until she was inside, and the door safely closed.

He turned and walked away, heading for the saloon where he was staying. His heart suddenly felt hollow knowing he would leave this delightful little town. Despite lying to himself, Caleb knew in his heart, Belle was the reason for his sadness. If he hadn't decided at the last minute to pop into the candy store and take a chance at selling more aprons, right before closing time, he would never had met her.

Sometimes the thing you need the most is right at your fingertips, but often times, the timing is off, and you simply have to walk away. Caleb repeated it in his head over and over until he reached his accommodations at the saloon. The rambunctious customers made him think of Belle and the way she'd described the saloon to him earlier. He'd had no choice since there were no other accommodations available as far as he could tell. He had tried, but couldn't find a boarding house, except one exclusively for single women. *Mrs. Potter's Rooms for Genteel Ladies* didn't seem quite appropriate for him. Caleb chuckled at his own joke, then climbed the stairs to his room.

He kicked off his boots, then lay down on top of the bed staring at the ceiling, hands clasped behind his head. He was tired of traveling all the time. After he left Bozeman, he would decide on his future. He'd made far more money than he would ever need as a single man. He had more than enough to purchase a house and settle down somewhere.

Somewhere like Dewberry perhaps.

He suddenly jumped up and strolled to the window. He needed to leave in the morning. The charming Miss Belle Armstrong was causing him to think in the most ridiculous of ways. Leaving Dewberry and making his way to Bozeman was the best thing he could do for all concerned.

He glanced out the window again. The snow was getting heavier; so much so, he could barely see outside now. With his horses safely stowed away at the livery, along with his wagon, Caleb decided to bed down for the night and forget he'd ever met his supper companion.

Instead, he'd tossed and turned most of the night, her pretty face darting into his vision every time he closed his eyes. He dreamed of holding her close, and of her luscious lips. Caleb wondered what it would be like to kiss her. In that moment, he knew it was imperative he leave Dewberry the moment the sun rose.

He needed to get out of there and far away from the enticing candy store owner.

Belle stood over the stove stirring the butter and sugar for the butterscotch candy she was making today. She'd planned to make it last night, but Caleb Bligh interfered with her plans. Not that she was complaining; she'd had a wonderful time.

She added the molasses and salt, stirring some more until all the ingredients were melted and completely combined. Then she brought it to the boil. It was hot work standing over the stove, making all the products she sold, but she marketed her candies as being hand made by her, and by golly, that's exactly what she would do.

Sometimes, as Christmas drew closer, and she got busier, Belle would hire someone to help. But finding the right person to handle the day-to-day sales, someone with experience, was the most difficult issue. Last year she'd employed Mary Hanson, and she'd worked out well. Mary had since married and was currently with child, so she was out of the question this year.

When the mixture began to sizzle, Belle glanced down at the large pot on the stove. She really needed to keep her mind on what she was doing. It had almost boiled over the sides, and what a mess that would have made!

Belle poured the sticky mixture into her prepared pans and put them aside for the butterscotch to set. It was a customer favorite, and Belle knew she'd be making more before the week was over.

Licorice was next on the agenda, but first she needed to clean up from the butterscotch. This was the part she disliked the most, but it had to be done. The method of making licorice was almost the same, but there were some additional ingredients. She reached for the condensed milk and anise, as well as the blackstrap molasses. Once again, when it was ready, Belle poured the mixture into the prepared tins to set.

Now that she'd caught up, Belle took a moment to catch her breath and make herself a cup of coffee. Sometimes it was all that kept her awake. Not that she didn't enjoy watching the sunrise, but a little more sleep would be most welcome.

As she brought the mug her to lips, Belle wondered what Caleb was doing right now. More likely than not, preparing to leave town. More's the pity – she did enjoy his company last night. She glanced up and stared out the window. It was snowing heavily. There was no way he could leave this morning, not in this weather. He probably wouldn't get to leave at all today unless the weather changed dramatically, and that was highly unlikely.

She finished her coffee, cleaned up the kitchen again, then breathed a sigh of relief. Now that that was done, and the licorice and butterscotch were almost set, she could busy herself in the store. With this cold weather, it wouldn't be long, and she would be able to finish off her freshly made candies. The thought made her smile. In the warmer weather, it took far longer for them to set.

She fetched some display trays from the store, ready to add those into her glass cabinet for customers to see the variety of goodies available to them. She worked hard and reaped the benefits of that hard work. She just wished she could afford to employ someone all year round and take the pressure off herself.

As soon as the thought entered her mind, Belle admonished herself. She should be incredibly grateful she had a store that was profitable. The Good Lord had been kind to her and helped her business to thrive. Without her faith, she had no idea where she would be now.

It was time to open the store. She removed her soiled apron and pulled one of her new aprons over her head. She'd no sooner lifted the blind to the door, than Caleb appeared on the other side.

"Good morning," he said, as she waved him inside. He was far more chipper than she'd expected, given he was stuck here for another day.

"Good morning to you too. Thank you again for last night, it was delightful."

He studied her, looking her up and down, and it made Belle feel a little uncomfortable. "You probably realized I couldn't leave today." He glanced outside and scowled at the heavy snowfall. "Perhaps tomorrow."

"You won't know until tomorrow. The weather is very unpredictable here in Dewberry." She continued to fuss about the store during their conversation, and Caleb stared at her.

"What can I do to help?"

She stopped what she was doing and straightened up. "Not a thing. I have it all under control, but thank you for the kind offer."

Belle had to continue what she was doing, or she wouldn't have everything ready when her customers began to arrive. This close to Christmas she knew there would be a steady stream of eager customers each day. There always was this time of year.

She straightened the candies in the window, then rearranged those in the cabinet to allow the new additions. He took two steps back and watched her work. It made Belle nervous, why she had no idea.

There was a tap on the door, and Belle glanced up. Mrs. Jensen was at the door, endeavoring to enter, but Caleb had the door blocked. "I do apologize," he said, as he opened the door for the customer.

"It is quite all right," she said in a huff, telling Belle it certainly wasn't all right in Mrs. Jensen's eyes. She wasn't the most forgiving woman at any time, let alone when she was stuck outside in the cold and the snow. She brushed snow from her coat and pulled off her thick gloves.

She stared into the glass cabinet. "Do you have any butterscotch, my dear?" This time her demeanor was far better.

Belle glanced up and smiled. "Freshly made this morning, but I'm afraid I haven't cut it yet. If you are prepared to wait a few minutes…"

"Of course!" Even when she wasn't in a huff, Mrs. Jensen sometimes sounded as though she was.

Belle hurried into the kitchen and began to cut the butterscotch for her impatient customer. Thank goodness she'd finished making it when she did. "How much did you want, Mrs. Jensen?" she called from the back, realizing too late it was most unladylike. Word was sure to spread around. The woman was one of the biggest gossips in town. Apart from Mrs. Grayson that was – but for the latter, her heart was in the right place.

"I'll take a small bag full, if you have enough."

Of course she had enough. Didn't she just tell the woman she'd spent the morning making it? Belle sighed. Mrs. Jensen was by far her most difficult customer, but there was no way she would show her frustration to her customer. Or to Caleb. As a salesman, he would surely have come across his own version of Mrs. Jensen. Belle cut and packaged the order.

"There you are. That will be fifty cents thank you, Mrs. Jensen."

The expression on the woman's face said it all. Despite her advantageous financial situation, Mrs. Jensen always balked when given a price. As though it was all the money she had in the world. Only Belle knew better. She could double her prices and still be reasonable compared to the big city stores, and some days Belle had contemplated doing just that. She silently counted to ten. Her annoyed customer dug into her reticule and handed over some coins, then turned on her heel and hurried out of the store without another word.

"Well, I never," Caleb commented once the door was closed.

Belle sighed. "I'm afraid I'm more than a little used to it.

Caleb frowned. "I've encountered the same on my travels, but not a lot. Most of the ladies are thrilled to have the opportunity to replenish their fading or threadbare linens." He studied her momentarily. "I see you are making the most of your purchases." He raised his eyebrows. Did he not expect her to wear them?

"Not that the likes of Mrs. Jensen appreciates it." She sighed again. Some days it felt like it was all for nothing. Fifty cents was a drop in the proverbial ocean for most of her customers. After all, if they couldn't afford the cost of her candies, they had no right frequenting her store. And that was the truth.

"Since I'm stuck here for another day, will you accompany me to lunch?"

Belle's heart did a little flutter. It wasn't like she knew the man standing in front of her, so why was she reacting like this. "Well…"

"Oh come on, you know you want to." He grinned at her, and for the first time she noticed the dimples on the sides of his face.

When she didn't answer straight away, he pretended to pout, causing Belle to burst out laughing. Caleb in turn, began to laugh. Tears of laughter rolled down her cheeks. She hadn't laughed so much in a very long time. Simply because there wasn't anything to laugh about.

He reached out and brushed her tears away. "Happy tears, I hope." He stared into her face, a worried expression on his face.

"Of course," she said, taking a step back. She shouldn't be standing here like this, allowing this stranger to touch her in such an intimate fashion. Belle glanced outside, hoping no one was about. She would be the talk of the town if they'd been seen. She breathed a sigh of relief there was no one there.

He studied her momentarily, then dropped his hands to his sides. "I apologize. I overstepped; I had no right to touch you like that."

What did she say to that? *It's all right?* It wasn't true, and Belle wasn't one to lie. "No, you didn't," she said quietly.

His head shot up and he stared at her. "Again, I apologize. I'll pick you up at noon for lunch."

Before she had an opportunity to respond, either to accept or refuse his invitation, Caleb Bligh was gone. The only indication he'd ever been there was the enticing aroma he left behind.

Chapter Three

Despite her resolve not to dine with Mr. Bligh, as she decided to call him – Belle's way of keeping the man at bay – she felt a flutter of excitement when the bell over the store's door tinkled at noon. She glanced up and he removed his hat and brushed the snow from his shoulder. "There's quite a storm out there," he said confidently, as though she had agreed to dine with him. *She hadn't, had she?*

Belle wasn't sure now and was quite confused. She shook herself mentally. How could one man, a stranger no less, make her feel this way? It wasn't as though she'd never been out with a man before, because she had. Although, to be honest, it was a long time ago, and they could hardly be called men. They were barely out of their teens. Now Caleb, er, Mr. Bligh, he was a man through and through.

"Oh for goodness sakes," she said abruptly. Out loud. Which was not what she had intended.

Mr. Bligh stared at her. "Are you all right, Belle? Did I miss something?"

She lifted her chin and stared right at him. "I am perfectly fine, thank you, *Mr. Bligh.*"

Confusion covered his face. Then his hand lifted and he scrubbed it across his chin. As though he chose to ignore everything that happened only moments ago, he reached for her coat that was hanging on the rack and held it out for her. Belle stared momentarily, then allowed him to help her into her coat. "It's freezing outside. I do hope you have gloves. And a scarf." He lifted his eyebrows quizzically, then pulled his own scarf around his neck a little tighter.

She pulled her gloves onto her hands, then turned to him. "I didn't bring my scarf today, but I will survive." She then headed toward the door.

Caleb deftly pulled his scarf from around his neck and held it out. Belle stared at him, then waved him away. "I told you, I'm fine. I'm quite used to this weather; you are not."

Before she knew what was happening, the scarf was around her neck, and his warmth seeped into her. The scent that was Caleb Bligh was suddenly part of Belle, and she breathed deeply. His fingers fiddled with the scarf, ensuring her neck was properly protected. He was so close to her that Belle felt a little overwhelmed. If he was any closer, their lips would be touching, and that simply wasn't right.

"That's better," he said quietly, and his warm breath touched her lips. She felt giddy, like a schoolgirl, which was absolutely crazy. It was almost as though he'd kissed her.

She stared into his eyes that were as brown as the chocolates she'd made the day before. And he stared into hers. It was like looking into a mirror. What were the chances they would both have brown eyes? *What color eyes would their children have, she wondered.*

The moment the thought hit her, she gasped. Caleb Bligh was leaving Dewberry the moment the weather cleared. They would part ways, and she would never see him again. She must keep that at the front of her mind, and not get caught up in the romance of it all.

He stared at her. "Everything all right?"

"Perfectly. We should leave for the diner soon, or I shan't have enough time to eat before I must open the store again."

Caleb reached over and turned the sign on the door to closed. He looked far too comfortable doing it, and it made Belle's heart thud. How many other women had he dined, and how many times had he turned the sign to closed? *Probably far more than she cared to know about.*

The moment he did it, Caleb realized what he'd done. He'd assumed it was fine for him to turn the store sign to closed, but the look of horror on Belle's face told him otherwise. It wasn't like he did it all the time. In fact, this was a first for him. Trouble was, he felt far too comfortable around this woman. Belle Armstrong made him feel far too relaxed and at ease. Usually he would take the ladies to supper the night before and be gone by morning. In this case, the force of nature dictated otherwise.

Basically, he had no choice.

Although, if he thought about it, he could have found another partner to dine with – there were plenty of elderly ladies around Dewberry. Truth was, he didn't want to find someone else. He was more than happy to dine with Belle, and seemingly, she with him.

He waited as she locked the door, standing three steps behind her. The last thing he wanted to do was crowd her or make her feel uncomfortable. It had been an incredible amount of time since Caleb had encountered someone he was interested in, and the shame of it all was he'd been gone soon. The last thing he wanted was to get her hopes up. Or his.

Belle turned to face him and pulled the collar up on her coat. His scarf flapped in the wind, and he reached out to capture it, then wrapped it around her neck again. The action felt far too intimate, and he suddenly pulled his hand away as if he'd been burned. She watched his every move, and Caleb felt like a schoolboy who'd been ogling a teenage girl he was interested in.

Only he wasn't a schoolboy, and she wasn't a teenager. They were both adults. So why did he feel like he'd done something wrong? "It's so cold," she said, her teeth beginning to chatter. "We need to get to the diner, and out of the cold."

"We do," he said, afraid if he kept talking he might say something he would later regret. Like *I really like you*, or *I don't want to leave here without you*, or even, *Will you marry me?* He couldn't believe how entrenched his feelings seemed to be. This was totally not like him. He normally arrived in a town, stayed the night, then left early next morning.

And that was exactly what he would have done had the weather not turned nasty. Only Caleb knew that might not be true. He had developed feelings for Belle almost from the moment he met her. The chemistry between them was breathtaking, and he couldn't believe how drawn to her he felt.

Finally, they arrived at the diner. He opened the door and ushered her inside. "Let me take your coat," he said before Merry, the owner of the diner, could do it. As his guest, it was his responsibility to take care of her. He'd be frightfully disappointed if that was taken from him.

As he pulled her coat from her, Caleb felt a thrill go up his arm. The last time they were skin on skin, the same thing happened. The warning signs were there – why didn't he take notice of them? He already knew the answer – because he didn't want to. He loved this little town he'd happened across, but more than that, he was drawn to its charming candy store owner.

Caleb knew it would be his undoing. The moment the weather cleared, he needed to leave. If it wasn't for the safety and well-being of his horses, he would have hightailed it out of Dewberry at first light. The last thing he needed in his life was a relationship. He spent his life traveling, selling his wares. He couldn't stay in one place more than a day or two; it simply wasn't practical.

"Is this table all right?" Merry's voice broke into his thoughts, and Caleb automatically agreed.

"We don't have long," he managed through the fog that was meant to be his brain. "Belle has to get back to open the store again."

"Of course," Merry said as she handed them each a menu. "The quickest item on the menu is thick beef and vegetable soup with freshly cooked hot rolls."

He glanced across at Belle who nodded her agreement. "Perfect. We'll both have the soup, thank you." Merry hurried away and left them alone. Caleb sat back in his chair and sighed. This was impossible. Between Belle's store responsibilities, and his business that was always on the move, a relationship simply wouldn't work. He glanced up at her, and Belle's eyes pierced his. He was getting way ahead of himself. There was no relationship, and there never would be. They were two souls passing like ships in the night. Tomorrow the weather would clear, and he would be gone from Dewberry forever.

Ordinarily, he would probably return in six months or so, but Caleb knew he couldn't return here again. Not ever. The pain of seeing Belle and knowing there could be nothing between them would be far too excruciating for him to bear.

"Here you are. Thick beef and vegetable soup with hot rolls."

"It smells delicious," Caleb said as he leaned in and absorbed the fragrance. He lifted his spoon and took a small mouthful. "Tastes delicious too – just like home cooked."

Merry smiled, then left them alone.

There was a comfortable silence between them as they ate, and he knew that wasn't a good thing. Caleb would much prefer an awkward silence as it would mean they were not at ease with each other. He scrubbed a hand across his clean shaven chin as he pondered the situation he found himself in.

On the one hand, he was so drawn to this woman he wanted to flee. On the other hand, he wanted to get to know her better. He stared out the window at the heavy snowfall and willed it to stop. Even if it was only long enough for him to reach his next destination. But Caleb knew that wasn't going to happen. Belle had told him as much. She'd said once that snow set in, there was no stopping it. His only option was to get used to it and be ready to leave when it was safe to do so.

He tore open his hot roll and reached for the butter sitting in the middle of the table. His fingers tingled as they brushed against Belle's as she also reached for the butter. He glanced up and smiled ever so briefly. She grinned.

It seemed Belle was thoroughly enjoying herself, when all he was doing was worrying over things he had no control over. "Sorry. You go first," he said quietly.

Belle stared at him momentarily. "Everything all right? You seem lost in thought."

She was far too intuitive for his liking. "Just thinking about how long I'm going to be stuck here." The words were out before he had the sense to think about them. Her smile suddenly turned into a frown. "Of course I would stay if I could, but…work." He couldn't dig himself in any deeper if he tried. Or could he? "Not that there's any other reason for me to stay." This time he earned himself a scowl. Caleb mentally slapped himself. Apart from the fact it was far from the truth, he'd hurt her feelings. "I didn't mean…"

She reached out and covered his hand. "It's all right," she said firmly. "We are but strangers."

Every word she said was truth, but it didn't help. Caleb felt deep regret at his uncensored words, and knew he'd hurt her. "I'll likely be leaving tomorrow," he said, trying to undo the harm he'd done.

Instead of the confirmation he expected, Belle laughed. "I highly doubt it," she said as she buttered a roll. "This weather has set in. Expect to be here at least another few days." Belle smiled, but Caleb inwardly screamed. The last thing he needed was to be stuck here in Dewberry, in close proximity to the charming Miss Armstrong.

As he accompanied her back to the store, they encountered some of the locals along the way. Belle introduced him to Mrs. Ethel Grayson, who she explained later, was the town busy-body and also an unofficial matchmaker.

"Please tell me it's not true," he said as they walked away. The last thing he needed was some stranger pushing them together. Keeping his distance was probably the hardest thing Caleb had ever had to do. Having a little old lady who didn't know him try to mold his future, did not seem to be in his best interest. Or Belle's for that matter.

Belle smirked at his comment. "It is clear you don't know Mrs. Grayson. She has already matched up some of the couples here on Dewberry Lane." Suddenly the smirk disappeared, and she went quiet. Was Belle as much against their being matched as he was?

Wasn't that what he wanted? If that really was the case, why did he feel so disheartened at her reaction?

Chapter Four

Caleb rushed into Candies Galore and out of the snow. Would this storm ever give up? More importantly, would he ever get to leave Dewberry? It wasn't that he wanted to leave per se, but he was growing far too attached. Not to the town itself, but the owner of one particular store. The one he was standing in right this moment.

Belle glanced up as the bell tinkled. "Oh! Come inside," she said as she helped him out of his coat. "You must be freezing. Come out the back and warm up."

It was the last thing Caleb expected, but he would take it. A chance to warm up by the fire was definitely welcome. "Thanks. I am rather cold." He pulled his thick gloves off, and Belle placed them with his coat. Not that you could tell looking at it, but his coat was quite warm. He was a man used to the elements all year round and planned for that. But this weather would have to be the worst he'd encountered. At least that he could recall.

Hands as close as he dare put them, Caleb stood in front of the fire, still shivering from the cold.

"I have coffee." She grinned then poured a mug of steaming coffee.

"I wouldn't say no to that either." He would have smiled if his face hadn't been frozen solid. Of course that was an exaggeration, but it certainly felt that way. He reached for the mug, and their hands collided. A shiver ran down his spine, and Caleb knew he was in deep trouble. Never in all his adult years had a woman affected him so much. Of course he had teenage crushes, but this didn't feel like a crush; it was far different.

When he wasn't with her, he craved the company of Belle. When he was with her, he wanted to pull her close and kiss her. These were things he knew he shouldn't be feeling or craving, and Caleb knew the only way to relieve himself of these urges was to leave Dewberry. Trouble was, he couldn't.

He was stuck here until the storm passed, and that could be a matter of hours, or if the locals were right, and they probably were, it could be days. He sighed, then sipped his coffee. "I don't have cupcakes or cookies here, but I made fresh fudge this morning." She held out a plate with a few enticing pieces of fudge on them.

He stared down at her offerings. "Looks and smells delicious. Don't mind if I do." How long had it been since he'd eaten freshly made fudge? "The last time I ate fudge, it was weeks old, and hard as a rock. I should visit Dewberry more often." The moment the words were out of his mouth, Caleb wanted to take them back. Once he left Dewberry, he knew he could never return. He couldn't go through this pain again. His heart was already hurting, knowing he had to leave.

He was convinced, more than ever, that he and Belle were meant to be together, but they each had their separate lives to live. His was on the road, traveling throughout Montana. Hers was here in this tiny town called Dewberry. A town he didn't even know existed until recently.

Caleb reached out and took a piece of the fudge. It was still slightly warm. "This is delicious. The best fudge I've ever eaten," he said, as it melted in his mouth. "But don't tell my sister that." He grinned then, the action making him feel far better, especially now he'd warmed up.

"She probably doesn't have my secret recipe," Belle said, her eyebrows raised.

"Secret recipe, huh?" He shrugged, indicating he didn't believe a word.

She reached for a tattered book hidden in a cupboard drawer. "From my grandmother," she said, tapping the notebook with one finger. "The fudge recipe came from my mother, but most of the other recipes have been passed down through generations."

"Ah, now I understand why your store is so popular." She looked rather deflated, so he expanded. "Candy making is a dying art. Very few people are able to create the delicacies you make." He leaned in closer. "You are an artiste, my dear." He grinned, and she laughed, a delightful sound that set his nerve endings on edge. Not because it annoyed him, but due to the complete opposite.

"I'd better get back to work. I will have customers streaming in here soon, wanting their daily fix." She laughed again, and he was hooked. That he should feel so enamored this soon after meeting this young woman, concerned him more than words could convey.

"What can I do to help?" The words were out before he had the forethought to stop them. "Not that I'm much of a candy maker." He shrugged. Caleb knew far more about candy making than he would let on.

She stopped dead and stared at him, her hands on her hips. Belle opened her mouth to speak, then closed it again. It left him wondering what she was about to say. She suddenly turned around and hurried out of the room.

Had she worked out his secret? Or did she simply need to get back to work? He would probably never know.

Caleb stood by the fire a little longer and finished his coffee. Then it was time to either help her out or leave. The last thing Caleb wanted was for the locals to have a reason to gossip. If Belle's words were anything to go by, Mrs. Grayson would gladly spread rumors about the two of them. Perhaps even try to push them into a corner and force marriage on them. He shuddered. He liked Belle, there was no doubt about that, but marriage was the last thing on his mind.

He washed the mug and hurried out into the store. Thankfully it was empty. Belle was rearranging her candies on the display trays when he entered. "Can I interest you in accompanying me for lunch today?"

She straightened up and studied him. "It's far too early for lunch."

He shrugged. "I've lost track of time with nothing to do all day. Maybe a coffee at the diner?" His voice sounded almost pleading, and Belle stared at him, pity written all over her face.

"I'm pretty organized, but I can probably find something." Almost the moment the words were out, the front door opened, and a delivery of boxes and other supplies arrived.

"Delivery for Miss Armstrong," the delivery man announced as he pulled a pencil out from behind his ear. "Sign here please." He handed the clipboard over, leaving the boxes in the path of Belle's customers. Right now, no one could get in the door to the store.

"Typical," she said under her breath. Her sigh was not lost on Caleb.

He lifted the box on top and stared pointedly at her. "Tell me where to put them, and consider it done."

"You don't have to. I am capable."

It was his turn to sigh. Why did she have to be so fiercely independent? Were men the big bad wolf in her eyes? "What else am I to do? I can't go anywhere."

She nodded and showed him where to leave the delivery. "Thank you," she said. "I do appreciate it." She smiled and warmth traveled from his head to his toes. If that was all it took for him to be happy, he was in big trouble.

It didn't take long for him to relocate the boxes out of the doorway, and once again, Caleb was at a loss of what to do. "Perhaps I can sweep the kitchen, or wipe down the benches? Anything you want to dish out. I am bored beyond comprehension."

He hoped his words would send some sympathy his way – enough Belle would put him to work, but instead she scowled. "My kitchen is spotless." Now she pouted, and Caleb thought perhaps it was best he leave.

He held up his hands in front of himself, grabbed his coat and gloves, and began to back out of the little store. "I didn't mean anything by it. I'll leave you to it, shall I?"

Hands on her hips, Belle watched his every move until he was out of Candies Galore. What he would do with the rest of the day, Caleb had no idea. He did know he was already cold to the bone, and he'd only been outside a matter of minutes. Before he knew it, he was heading toward *Ma's Diner*. Merry's had become the friendly face he needed in his time of forced isolation from the rest of the world.

Caleb hugged the hot mug of coffee as he stared out the window. Rather than petering off, the snow appeared to be getting heavier.

Belle had not given him a definitive answer either way about lunch. She only told him it was too early to eat. Perhaps he could check again later? He shook his head – it might not be such a good idea, especially if she thought he was becoming a nuisance. Caleb understood her reasoning for keeping him at bay – it was the surely same argument he'd had with himself. Getting to know the candy store owner was a terrible idea. In a day or so, he'd be gone from Dewberry, and she would be quite alone once more.

From his own perspective, he was becoming far too fond of Belle. He'd known from the moment he met her they had clicked. Their chemistry was obvious. At least it was to Caleb, and he therefore assumed it was to Belle too.

"Belle busy today?" Merry's voice brought him out of his reflections.

Caleb glanced up. She looked more confused than anything. "She said she was behind with preparing for Christmas." He placed the coffee mug on the table, and Merry refilled it for him. "But I don't think that's true." He stared down into his lap and expected the diner's owner to quietly slip away, but she didn't.

"Did you argue?" She seemed genuinely concerned.

He studied her before answering again. "Quite the contrary. I think that's the problem."

Instead of leaving him alone, Merry slipped into the seat opposite him. "Belle likes you," she said quietly. "And I can tell you like her too. I've watched you both when you're together." A sly smile slid across her face.

He glanced at her momentarily, then licked his lips. "Is it really that obvious?"

It was Merry's turn to study him. "It's that noticeable." She stood as the door to the diner swung open and a group of customers entered. "Do something about it now, or you will both regret it." With that, she turned and headed toward the customers who waited at the door.

Caleb had a lot of thinking to do, but had no idea how he was going to get out of this with his heart intact. Before he could ponder his situation further, he was joined by his new acquaintance, Mrs. Grayson.

"Hello, Mr. Bligh. I see we meet again. Do you mind?" She'd already taking the liberty of sitting opposite him, so even if he did, it was far too late. Mrs. Grayson waved a hand, and Merry joined them.

"Mrs. Grayson, what can I get for you?" Merry plonked a mug in front of the older woman, and filled it with steaming hot coffee. "The usual?"

"Thank you, Merry, that would be wonderful. Enough for two, if you don't mind." Caleb's head shot up. "Oh, don't protest, Mr. Bligh. I can't eat alone, and you're far too skinny for this weather." The old lady laughed at her own joke, and Caleb couldn't help but join her. He was no doubt nervous with Mrs. Grayson after what Belle said about her being the town matchmaker, but she seemed friendly enough.

"I wouldn't dream of refusing such a generous offer," he said, even if it was said in jest. It wasn't long before Merry returned with a plate of warm biscuits with jam and cream. "They look delicious," he said, rubbing his hands together. "If you only knew how long it has been since I've indulged in such a delicacy."

When he glanced up, his companion was studying him. "What's your story, Mr. Bligh?"

He felt like an insect under a microscope and had to resist squirming in his seat. After all, isn't that what she wanted? For him to feel uncomfortable. "The name is Caleb. I'm a traveling salesman, and offer a range of linen goods to stores as well as direct to consumers at markets."

"I see." She said the words as though he was the worst of the worst. "Well, Mr. Bligh, it doesn't sound as though your prospects are particularly good." Mrs. Grayson sat with her arms crossed and a scowl on her face. She addressed him as though he had just asked for his girlfriend's hand in marriage, and she was the father of the prospective bride.

He had just taken a mouthful of coffee, and it took all his effort not to splutter and cover the woman in the hot brown substance. He reached for the linen napkin sitting on the table, one of his if he wasn't mistaken, and wiped his mouth with it. It gave him time to compose himself. Should he try to form an answer, or just ignore her words? Something told him this was a woman not to be ignored. "I guess that depends on your perspective," he said choosing his words very carefully. "For a single man with no family to support, it's an excellent job. For a married man, probably not so much. There's a lot of travel involved."

Caleb now crossed *his* arms and sat back in his seat. He stared at his companion and watched as her face completely transformed into a grin. "I expect you must get lonely." Her eyebrows rose, and the grin became wider.

He was once again on edge. Belle was right – the woman was set on matching them up. He mentally slapped himself. Caleb stared out the window at the snow that was getting heavier by the hour.

"Oh, you won't be leaving anytime soon, Mr. Bligh," she said, insisting on addressing him more formally. "This weather reminds me of the last blizzard we endured here in Dewberry – I believe it was in sixty-five. No, it might have been sixty-six. Either way, it was ghastly. We couldn't leave our homes for days." She winked at him then. "Eat up, Mr. Bligh, before your biscuits get cold."

Why all of a sudden did Caleb feel like this was his last meal?

Chapter Five

Long after Mrs. Grayson left the diner, Caleb stayed right where he sat. He skulked about drinking coffee and wishing the snow would clear. But of course it wouldn't. If anything, it would get far worse. That fact had been confirmed far too many times by way too many people – to the point his situation felt hopeless.

When customers began to flow in for the lunchtime rush, he decided it was time to leave. Belle had to eat sometime – the trick would be trying to convince her to dine with him. The strangest thing had happened since he'd arrived in the tiny town, and he had no way to explain it. Caleb felt lonelier now than he'd ever felt. Even stranger, when he spent time with Belle, the feeling disappeared.

As he shrugged his coat on before leaving the diner, Caleb halted. Surely that didn't mean what he thought it meant? He'd only known Belle for a matter of days. He shook his head trying to chase away the thought – it was clearly built of boredom. There was nothing for him to do here, and Caleb was not a man used to lingering about without a purpose. If only he could get Belle to let him help. Unfortunately, the young woman was far to proud to let a complete stranger help her. Or should one say she was far too intelligent? She didn't know him from Adam, or what he might do to ruin her business. Not that Caleb had any such thoughts, but she did not know that.

He flipped his collar up around his neck to keep out the icy bite of the snow. He'd traveled to a lot of places, but never had he encountered chill such as he felt here. It was enough to make a man want to leave. If he could leave, that was, which he couldn't, not without endangering his horses and himself.

Caleb made his way to Candies Galore. The walk back seemed far more difficult than earlier. When he looked down, he discovered the reason – the snow was six inches deep, and he was struggling to walk. His mind had been elsewhere; he'd been doing that far too often lately. Idle hands had also affected his mind. Or perhaps the thoroughly disarming Mrs. Grayson had a part in that as well. She might be a matchmaker, but from what Belle told him, she was also a very kind old lady, one who looked out for those in need. The thought made him smile. The world needed more people like her, but please Lord, put her matchmaking skills to rest until he could leave Dewberry.

He finally made it to the store. Getting the door open was an entirely different situation. Snow was packed high here as well, making it difficult to pull the door open. Using his boot-covered feet, Caleb pushed it aside, then opened the door and went inside. "Is it usually this bad?"

Belle turned to face him. "Not very often," she said, wiping her hands on her embroidered apron. "But we're in for a blizzard. This is nothing compared to what we will get."

His heart thudded. Surely she was joking. Although when he thought about it, Mrs. Grayson also mentioned a blizzard, although not so directly.

"You've never been in one?"

He shook his head vigorously. "No, and I'd hoped to keep it that way."

"No such luck. The kettle is on if you would like coffee?"

It was the last thing he wanted after spending almost the entire morning in the diner doing nothing *but* drink coffee. "Thanks but no thanks. I came to take you to lunch." She opened her mouth to protest, but he stopped her before she had a chance to say no. "Oh, and I met up with Mrs. Grayson this morning. You were correct – she's trying to match us up."

Belle went pale. *Was he really that bad?* "The woman interrogated me. Can you believe that?"

Belle laughed and color returned to her face. "I definitely can. She's incorrigible when it comes to matchmaking."

His heart sank. As much as he liked Belle, he would like the choice of partner – if he ever decided to marry that was. He hated the thought of someone else choosing for him, especially someone who barely knew him. Mrs. Grayson had spent less than an hour with Caleb, so had no idea of who he was, or the type of woman he liked.

Heck, he had no idea of sort of woman he was interested in. It had been close to a decade since he'd dated, and that had been a disaster. Martha Templeton had been all over him, trying to ruin her reputation and force Caleb into a situation where he had no choice but to marry her. He saw right through the floosy, and would have none of it. He'd been on the road ever since.

But Belle – she was the complete opposite, keeping her distance at all times, and pushing him away figuratively speaking, whenever possible. It finally occurred to him it was likely the reason she refused his help at all costs. She was certainly a woman, that given time to get to know properly, he would happily spend time with. Heck, the little time he'd spent with her already only enticed him further.

"The diner is filling up, so I thought we should leave soon."

She stared at him then, studied him closely. "And you know this how?"

Did he dare admit he'd sat there almost the entire morning because he had nothing else to do? "I, um…"

She nodded then, as though she could see right through him. "You really are bored, aren't you?" Belle sighed. "I suppose if you're *that* desperate, I can probably find something for you to do around here."

His heart thudded. On the one hand he welcomed the opportunity to fill in his time. On the other hand, it would mean spending far more time with Belle, and that might not be in his best interest. As he opened his mouth to respond, the door suddenly swung open, then quickly shut again.

"Mrs. Grayson! What are you doing here? I thought you'd be home keeping safe and warm by now."

A slow smile crossed the matchmaker's face as she glanced at him. It sent a shiver down Caleb's spine. *What was the old girl up to now?*

"I wanted to ensure you were safe. You need to put a shovel out front; it's packed with snow. I didn't think I would even get inside."

She sounded exasperated, and Caleb fully understood her frustration. "It was packed when I tried to get inside too," he said, sounding as frustrated as he felt. "I was just trying to convince Belle to dine with me."

The old lady's eyebrows rose, but she said nothing. Caleb and Belle shared a glance. Did Belle realize how desperate her customer was to match them? He dared not tell her the content of their conversation in case Belle decided to push the issue, but she didn't seem the type to force herself on a man.

He inwardly slapped himself. Belle was not like that. She'd had every opportunity to do so over the past days, but not once had she tried.

"This poor man is bored, Belle. There must be something you can give him to do? No one wants to be idle for days on end." She suddenly turned to face Caleb, a finger to her chin. "You're not of the Helena Bligh's are you? I once visited Jeremy Bligh's candy store. Oh, I guess it was decades ago now," she said, seemingly ready to go off on a tangent.

Caleb's heart pounded. He couldn't lie, so had to confess. "Jeremy Bligh was my father. Unfortunately, he is long gone."

Her face lit up. "Well it's a delight, I must say. Your father was one of the best, if not *the best* candy maker in Montana. How did you not know this,

Belle? This young man would have apprenticed under his father." She turned to face Caleb, and he felt heat travel up his face. He had decided not to disclose his identity to Belle for a reason. He didn't want her to feel obligated to allow him to cook for her store. Now the cat was out of the bag, she likely would.

"You're a candy maker? Why didn't you say something?" Her voice was accusing. She was obviously annoyed with him for not disclosing the information. She suddenly stormed off toward the kitchen.

Now he was annoyed – at Mrs. Grayson for telling his secret. Why didn't she ask him privately while they were at the diner? "I apologize," she suddenly said. "It only just occurred to me, and I should have spoken to you about it first. I didn't think." She sighed. "I often don't think; people tell me that all the time. I should know better by now." She shook her head as if further admonishing herself.

"It's all right. It was bound to come out sooner or later." And it was. Belle would have eventually realized, he was certain. Any candy maker worth their salt would know of Jeremy Bligh and his reputation. "At least now she might let me help out." He managed to smile, although the last thing he felt like doing was smiling. This might have put a rift between himself and Belle. But then again, didn't he want to keep his distance?

"Your father was a wonderful chocolatier and candy maker. What about you?" she asked pointedly. "Belle could certainly use your skills in that area. It's one thing that's sadly lacking in this store."

"What is lacking?"

Mrs. Grayson turned a bright shade of red. "I was just asking Mr. Bligh about his chocolate making skills. His father was well known in that area as well."

Belle turned to him and glared. Was it because he hadn't disclosed any of this, or because Mrs. Grayson had pointed out a deficit in her store?

"I can make chocolates. You've tasted them." She directed her statement at the elderly woman.

"And they are magnificent. Jeremy Bligh made *flavored* chocolates." Belle stared at her for long moments, then turned her attention to Caleb.

"Well," Belle said, her foot tapping impatiently. "Is that something you can do?" From the expression on her face, she was quietly fuming about his lack of admission regarding his skills. He wondered if it was born of frustration, or she truly was angry with him.

"I'm afraid so. I apprenticed with my father from the moment I was old enough. When he died, I didn't want anything to do with it again."

"Oh, that's a pity," Mrs. Grayson said, glancing from one to the other. "But then again, you two would never have crossed paths." Belle gasped, and Caleb held his tongue. As though she understood the sudden cold atmosphere surrounding them, the elderly lady continued. "I'm guessing you sold the store?"

"We did, not long after father died. I started my linen business with the proceeds. My sister Meg bought a house."

Mrs. Grayson leaned in closer. "Did you sell the recipes with the store?" Her voice was low, almost conspiratorial. It was clear to Caleb where this was going.

"That wasn't part of the deal. If you're asking can I use father's recipes here in Dewberry, the answer is yes. Part of my inheritance was his recipes."

"That is wonderful," Belle suddenly said brightly.

He let out the breath he'd been holding. Was Belle asking him to help out in the store. "You want me to cook for you? What happens when I leave?"

Mrs. Grayson stepped closer. "But that won't happen, dear boy. It is perfectly clear to me that you two are perfectly matched." And with those words spoken, a sly grin crossed her face, and the old lady left the store, leaving them staring after her.

Chapter Six

Lunch had been rushed, as Belle was keen to get back to the store and take advantage of Caleb's skills. "I can't pay you," she suddenly said, as they approached Candies Galore.

"I'm not asking you to. I am not a man used to sitting idly to pass the time of day. My mind is wandering all over the place as the minutes tick away. I'm afraid I'll go stark raving mad if I don't do something, and soon."

She chuckled, and the sound sent his heart fluttering. What a wonderful sound it was.

He shook himself mentally. Caleb was determined not to let Belle get under his skin, but he was terribly afraid it was already too late. It seemed that the clever matchmaker was determined to make it happen no matter what. If he was honest with himself, Caleb was attracted to Belle, but marriage was not on his agenda.

They entered the store, and Caleb headed for the kitchen. "Show me the ingredients you have, and I'll work out what I can make." He scanned each cupboard as Belle pointed him in the right direction. His eyes suddenly opened in excitement. "You have the ingredients for chocolates. Why is that, when according to Mrs. Grayson, you never make them?"

Guilt crossed her face. "They were delivered here accidentally. I wrote to the company, but they never returned to collect them. They told me to simply keep them."

"I guess it was cheaper for them that way." Caleb ran a hand through his hair. "Shall we start with chocolates then? A special Christmas treat for your fussy customers?"

She chuckled again and Caleb decided he liked it when she was happy. It lit up her entire face and sent warmth coursing through his body. For the first time, he decided being waylaid by a snowstorm might not be such a terrible thing after all.

He pulled the boxes down from the overhead cupboard. Luck was on his side as the shipment even included the molds and flavorings for the chocolates he planned to make. He snatched up an apron and pulled it over his head. "I don't suppose you have nuts? Father's nut chocolate bars were a big hit back in Helena."

Her eyes opened wide. "Nuts in chocolate? I've never heard of such a thing." She sounded affronted, but nonetheless pushed a pencil and paper toward him. "Anything you need, write it down. I'll visit the mercantile and see if they have it in stock."

Large pan in hand, Caleb reached for the pencil. "While you do that, I'll start with gum drops, shall I?"

Excitement lit up her face. "Oooh, my customers are going to be so excited."

"Until I leave, and they're back where they started." It wasn't something he wanted to think about, but it was the reality of the situation. And something they both had to accept. She stared at him, then nodded. Moments later he heard Belle lock up the store as she left.

That way he wouldn't be disturbed. Besides, she wouldn't be gone very long. It had been an incredibly long time since he'd done any of this. Did he still have what it took to produce quality candy? If he didn't, Belle would be sorely disappointed. He wouldn't put it past Mrs. Grayson to spread the word, so the pressure was on. His heart thudded as he began to panic – the last thing he wanted was to let Belle down.

Caleb took some deep breaths and calmed himself. This wasn't an emergency, he wasn't in the middle of a crisis; he was simply being asked to make candy. It was, after all, what he'd been trained to do. Granted it was a long time ago, but not far enough back he could no longer do it. He stumbled across the room and took a long drink of water. He even splashed water on his face, the coldness of it making him more alert.

He reached for the paper and pencil again, and began to write down the recipes he recalled, afraid he might forget. Worst case scenario, he would telegraph his sister. The original recipes were at her house for safe keeping. His only concern was if a fire should start there. She assured him more than once they would be the first thing she reached for if that were to happen. The recipes were priceless and could not be replaced.

Luckily, the majority were stored in his head, and he would be extremely grateful if he remembered them all.

For now, he would work on the gum drops. They were a relatively simple recipe but took some time to set. If he started on them now, they would be ready for sale in the morning. Caleb set about finding the ingredients and worked his way through the cupboards. Sugar, gelatin, flavorings, and coloring. He found some molds too – they weren't perfect for gum drops, but close enough. It wasn't the sort of mold you would generally have on hand. They were specific to that candy. If he was to hang around long enough, Belle might feel it was worthwhile to invest in the correct molds, but he would be gone in a few days, so it was pointless even thinking about it.

With cold water measured into the largest bowl he could find, he poured the gelatin over the top, then turned his attention to the pot he'd secured for this recipe. Again measuring out water, and this time adding sugar to the mix, he scurried about the kitchen checking out other available ingredients while the water came to the boil, stirring occasionally.

As he went about his business, it occurred to Caleb he was really enjoying himself. He hadn't thought about it much, but now realized how much he'd missed the candy making business. It had always given him a lot of satisfaction, and he'd assumed it was because he was working side by side with his father. Now he pondered the fact it might have been he simply enjoyed making candy, with his father or not.

A sudden sadness overtook him. He really did miss Father, but knew he'd be proud of Caleb helping out a fellow candy maker who needed his help. He shook himself mentally. She was helping him. He was the one who was bored, not Belle. He turned to the stove and stirred the syrup mixture, ensuring it didn't stick. It needed to simmer for at least five minutes. He would know when it was ready; he'd done this enough times to know by now. He leaned forward and breathed in. He'd always loved the sickly sweet smell of gum drops.

He startled as he heard the tinkle of the shop door. "I'm back," Belle called, and his heart fluttered at the sound. How did you miss someone you barely knew? He pushed the thought aside and continued preparing for when the syrup was ready to be taken from the stove. "Oh." She scanned the room, taking in what Caleb had been doing. "You've been busy."

"Gum drops," he said, then turned and stirred the syrup mix again. This part of the process was crucial. If it stuck or burned, it was useless and would have to be thrown away. He'd made a large batch and had no intention of wasting ingredients Belle had paid for. "Stand back," he demanded. "This is hot and dangerous."

Belle took a few steps back and Caleb carried the hot syrup to the table and poured it over the gelatin mixture. He then stirred until it was fully dissolved. He would leave it to cool somewhat, then divide into separate bowls before coloring and flavoring each one. The longest part of the process was leaving it to set after they'd been added to the molds. It was so cold they would likely be set late tonight and would be available for sale in the morning.

He leaned back on the counter behind him and breathed a sigh of relief. "It's been far too long, and I was afraid I wouldn't get the measurements right."

"But you did." Belle grinned, and his heart fluttered. Again. What was it about Belle that made him feel like a lovesick teenager?

"Indeed I did. What about the nuts? Did the mercantile have any?"

Now she grinned. "They did." She shoved a paper bag toward him, and Caleb snatched it up. He opened it and breathed in the aroma. "They're fresh too." He raised his eyebrows when Belle grinned.

"You don't think I'd buy inferior ingredients, do you? My customers are very fussy, as I'm sure you've noticed." She broke down into a laugh, and he joined her. He hadn't been this happy in a very long time.

Suddenly a shiver went down his spine. Did that mean what he thought it meant?

Old lady Grayson must be getting under his skin.

Belle scanned the room. The kitchen of Candies Galore was filled with gum drops and a variety of chocolates. She took a deep breath – it smelled heavenly. What would her customers say when they came to the store tomorrow? She could only imagine.

The snowstorm had been unforeseen, and unwanted, but meeting Caleb as a result, had been a blessing. She had never been overly religious, but she believed in God and her faith, and also fate. In her mind, everything that had happened over the past days was meant to be. If he hadn't decided to go off the beaten track and take a chance on Dewberry, she would never have met him.

Caleb stood back and studied his handiwork. A smile spread across his face, and a spark of lightning shot through Belle's heart. How did a mere smile cause such a reaction? She brushed the thought away. She was a confirmed spinster, and had no intention of marrying. Ever.

Not that anyone had asked her, nor would she accept, but for some crazy reason she felt a connection with Caleb Bligh. She shook herself mentally. It was that darned Mrs. Grayson, she'd planted an idea in her head, and now it wouldn't let go. Darn it.

"We'll have to think about what other candies you would like in the store." He looked so relaxed and so happy standing there, leaning against the counter, and it made her feel relaxed too. Suddenly the bell over the door tinkled.

"Hellooooo." It was Mrs. Grayson. *Why wasn't the woman tucked up safely at home, away from the storm?*

"Mrs. Grayson! I thought you'd be well home by now."

She grinned. "I decided to hang about town and find out what Mr. Bligh made." She craned her neck trying to see into the kitchen, but the store was planned in such a way customers couldn't see any mess that might be around. "Surely a valued customer such as myself is entitled to a sneak peek?"

Without waiting for confirmation or an invitation, she hurried toward the kitchen. "Oh my, it smells delicious," she said, taking in the aroma. "You have done your father proud, Mr. Bligh," she added. "When will these be available for me to purchase?"

"Tomorrow morning, and not a moment sooner." Belle was determined not to be coerced into letting her customer buy them earlier. Everything needed to set completely before they were sold.

"They're not completely set yet, Mrs. Grayson," Caleb said. "But if you don't mind that, you can have a small sample to tide you over." The old lady's face lit up. That was utter genius on Caleb's part. And it put an idea into her head – since these were new to the store, should they have a small sampling available to customers to entice them to buy?

"Oh my." The old lady was in heaven. The look on her face was one of pure bliss and sent warmth soaring through Belle. She could not believe her luck with Caleb. He would be such an asset to her store. Except… Except he would leave Dewberry in a matter of days. Her heart thudded.

"That first one was peppermint chocolate. Try this one," he said, pushing another sample toward her. "This is chocolate almond bar."

Mrs. Grayson winked. "That was one of your father's specialties if I recall correctly?" She took the proffered sample and again her expression was one of pure bliss. "I do hope you made plenty of these offerings. You will sell out in no time. I am putting in my order now, so *I* don't miss out! That would be an absolute catastrophe."

Then she eyed the gum drops. "Gum Drops! My absolute favorite. Dare I request a sample of those too?"

They were still a sticky mess. Caleb laughed, then rolled one in sugar, and finally handed over a sample.

"My boy, you are a genius." She glanced from Caleb to Belle. "You hold onto this one, my girl. You two are a perfect match." She pushed them together. "You look perfect together too." Belle huffed, then handed Mrs. Grayson a face cloth to clean up her hands.

She went on to give Belle her order, which included some of every flavor of each candy. Belle's costs were covered just from their uninvited visitor's order. Everything else would be pure profit.

"That went well," Caleb said once they were alone again.

"Indeed it did," Belle said, then brushed at her face. It felt as though something was there, but she couldn't move it.

"Here, let me," Caleb said, taking a step toward her. His hand lifted to her shoulder to steady her, and his other hand gently wiped her cheek. "You have chocolate stuck there," he said quietly, his voice suddenly husky and his eyes hooded. Belle's heart thudded. His headed slowly moved down until their lips almost met. He hesitated, perhaps to give her a chance to deny him, but when she didn't say no, his lips covered hers.

His arms came up around her, and he pulled her closer. Belle's heart pounded, and a shiver went down her spine. Little did she know when a hawker came to sell her his linens, that her life would be forever changed.

Chapter Seven

The new candies were far more popular than either Caleb or Belle had anticipated, and they sold out within the hour. It was quite obvious Mrs. Grayson had spread the word, because customers began flowing in minutes after the store opened. Caleb was convinced they would have queued outside before the doors opened had it not been snowing and icy cold.

He'd cut up a portion of the chocolates and candies for samples as Belle requested, which proved to be a massive hit. He couldn't recall if his father had done the same thing, but he wasn't involved in the sales part of the process, and simply didn't know. But knowing what a keen businessman his father was, it was highly likely.

Still smarting from *that kiss* last night, Caleb kept his distance. Neither of them had mentioned it, and likely, neither of them would. He had taken liberties he had no right to take, and they both knew it. He wasn't complaining; Belle was a beautiful woman with an appealing personality. He could do worse.

Not that he was looking for a wife. Oh no, that was the last thing Caleb wanted. Besides, he had a business where he was traveling constantly. That was not a life meant for a married man. However… if he did want to get married, Belle would be a perfect match for him.

Caleb shuddered. Where on earth were these thoughts coming from? One kiss and he'd turned to mush? Best he busy himself making more chocolates and candies before his brain turned to slop as well. He reached for the ingredients and got to work. Better to think about what he was making than the enticing woman standing out in the store. The woman who made his heart flutter every time she came close to him. The same one he couldn't stop thinking about when they were apart.

He growled out loud. *"This has got to stop!"*

"What has to stop?" Her sweet voice suddenly permeated the air, and he felt heat travel up his face.

What should he say? *That he'd been thinking about her and nothing else? When he was meant to be starting on a new batch of chocolates? Not the best idea he could come up with.* "Just me dallying instead of getting on with it."

"You don't have to do this you know."

"It gives me something to do, for which I'm rather grateful."

She didn't say a word, but instead flicked through the recipes he'd written down. "Everything is almost sold out." He could see her mind ticking over. It was as though he could read her thoughts – what would she do once he was gone? He would happily leave her the recipes. They were his to do whatever he wanted with them. He could even sell them, if that's what he decided to do, but he'd never do that. His father had entrusted Caleb with his life's work, and he had far too much respect for Jeremy Bligh to sell his secret recipes.

"I'm going to miss you when you leave," she said quietly. He could easily have missed her comment because it was barely above a whisper. When he glanced up, sadness etched her face.

"I'm going to miss you too." He took a few steps forward until he stood directly in front of her. Without thinking, his arms went up, and his head came down. He kissed her gently at first, but then it was far more thoroughly. *What was he doing?* He wasn't staying, couldn't stay, and kissing Belle was giving her false hope that he might hang around. Not temporarily, but forever.

He suddenly pulled back and stared into her face. "I'm sorry. I had no right…"

"I'm not complaining," she said, then licked her lips. Despite knowing it was wrong to take this woman in his arms and kiss her, he did it again. When he stopped, she rested her head against his shoulder and sighed. "I can't bear knowing you will leave soon." Tears shimmered in her eyes. "But we both know you have to leave when the blizzard is over."

His hands roamed over her back. It was meant to comfort Belle, but it worked just as effectively on him. "I do," he said quietly, regrettably, then pushed himself away. "And I need to get to work if you are to have more delights ready for your customers in the morning."

She threw him a tentative smile, then returned to the store. Away from temptation. Away from him.

When Belle returned, it was to say it was almost closing time. He had no idea where the day had gone, but the work bench was covered with a variety of chocolates, since those seemed incredibly popular. He'd also made candy apples and ribbon candy. They were always favorites in his father's store.

It would remain to be seen how popular they were in Candies Galore. Rock Candy was also popular back in Helena, so that was another consideration. He would discuss it with Belle and see what she wanted to do.

When he glanced up, she was pulling her apron over her head. "Time to go home," she said, keeping her distance. At first he felt hurt, then realized it was for the best. They were both becoming far too fond of each other. Again, Mrs. Grayson's doing. The woman had a lot to answer for.

Caleb sighed. It couldn't all be blamed on the matchmaker. She had been correct pushing them together – they were a perfect match, and no one could deny it. Not Belle, nor himself.

The question was, what were they to do about it? Leaving would be the obvious choice, but right now, that option had been taken out of his hands. Instead they would have to ride it out, and simply keep their distance.

~*~

Belle arrived early the next morning to place all the new candies on trays. She'd washed the trays last night before leaving, and Caleb had helped. He refused to leave until she was finished, but declined to stand idly by. The man was worth his weight in gold.

It was a pity he wouldn't be staying long-term, but Belle completely understood he had to move on, even if it did break her heart.

She soon heard a knock on the door. Belle couldn't believe it – customers were getting more assertive by the day wanting to see what new goodies were available to purchase. Caleb had certainly been a boon to her business. Wiping her hands on the clean apron she wore, Belle headed out to the shop. She pulled up the blinds that indicated the store was closed and came face-to-face with Caleb. Her heart fluttered.

What was he doing here this early? There was at least another hour to go before the store opened. *Surely he had other things to do with his time.* But of course, he didn't, and she knew it. It was the sole reason he'd ended up working in her store, creating a variety of candies and other delicacies. Her customers weren't complaining, and if she was honest with herself, neither was Belle.

She continued to stand there, staring at Caleb through the glass. Her mind was wandering, and she couldn't stop it. So many thoughts crossed her mind at that moment. Until he tapped on the glass again. "Are you going to let me in out of the cold, or stand there staring?" He had a smile on his face despite shivering in the snow.

She pulled the door ajar and let him pass. "Sorry, I was miles away."

"Apparently. I hope that stove of yours is good and hot. My hands are like ice blocks."

She frowned. "I really am sorry." Belle hurried through to the kitchen and opened the front of the stove and stirred it up. She left it open to warm the kitchen quickly.

"I know. Don't be sorry." It must have done the job, because soon Caleb took off his gloves, scarf, and coat. "What shall I make today? Something different or would you like a repeat of one of the candies I've already made?"

"Surprise me?" She was teasing him, but she didn't care. Caleb was so easy to get on with, and she was enjoying having someone else in the store to talk to for a change. It did get rather lonely there all day by herself, she had to admit. And that was despite the customers who came through her door during the course of the day.

Caleb's eyebrows lifted, then a sly smile crossed his face. "All right, I will then." He chuckled and turned his back to pull down ingredients from the nearby cupboard.

"What was it like growing up in a candy store?" Belle asked as she made them both a mug of coffee. It had become their daily routine – start the day sharing a coffee – and Belle wasn't complaining. She enjoyed the company. *Or was it Caleb's company specifically?*

He chuckled again. "Father was strict. We were limited to one item each day, and not until after school. Meg, my sister, tried to trick Father's staff into giving her more, but they risked their jobs, and did not comply to her demands." He began to pour sugar into a large pot. "She was too young to understand."

She watched with interest, wondering what he was making. "But you weren't?"

"We are several years apart in age." He added cornstarch to the sugar and mixed well. Next went in butter, corn syrup, salt, and water. Caleb then placed the entire mixture on the stove. She had no idea what he was making. Caleb stood at the stove stirring the concoction, then left it to reach for food coloring and flavoring. He then added them to the mix, stirring yet again.

Next he scrubbed the work bench. "I washed that last night," she said. "It's perfectly clean." She felt affronted, but at the same time, knew Caleb would have his reasons.

He suddenly reached for a large flat pan, and poured the entire mixture into it, then set it onto the work bench. His coffee sat untouched on the countertop, and finally he reached for it. He took a long sip, then sighed. "I needed that," he said. "The coffee at the saloon is awful." He pulled a face.

Belle had never been to the saloon, and had no intention of ever visiting there, but she could imagine. Coffee would not be something they sold a lot of. He stood drinking his coffee, not saying a word, but constantly watching the concoction he'd previously poured into the pan. Finally, after about ten minutes he put down his empty mug and laid a hand over the top. "Perfect. If you don't want to know what I'm making, you may want to leave the kitchen," he said, a hint of laughter in his voice.

"Oh for goodness sakes. It's *my* kitchen," she said in a huff, and stormed out.

"Your choice," he called after her, leaving no doubt about the laughter now. Not only was he teasing her, he knew exactly what he was doing. Belle was intrigued about what he was making and couldn't wait to see what it was. She fiddled about with the trays, rearranging and straightening the candies that were left on each tray from the previous day, and adding the candies she put on the trays this morning. These past days had been exciting – offering up new candies on a daily basis had given her little store new life. It had given her new purpose, and that made her incredibly happy.

Once the trays were all lined up in the glass cabinet, she couldn't wait any longer – she quietly moved toward the kitchen, and stood on the edge of the doorway, silently watching Caleb work. It was delightful. The man was a magician with candies, and she felt a tinge of jealousy. What she wouldn't do to become his apprentice!

Suddenly he glanced up, then mock scowled. "I thought you didn't want to know." He didn't stop pulling at the mixture until the color had changed from translucent to opaque. Then he rolled it into a long strip and reached for a large knife. Finally he began to cut it into pieces. "I need something to wrap each piece into," he said, glancing up at her and grinning.

"Taffy!" she suddenly shouted. "You're making taffy!"

He laughed out loud then. "No, I've made taffy. Do you think your customers will like it?"

"They will love it," she said, her heart fluttering again. Against her better judgement, Belle moved closer and covered his hand. A shiver ran down her spine and she tried to ignore it. "Thank you. I appreciate what you're doing for me," she said. Her voice was full of emotion, and he stared at her. *Did he guess she was beginning to have feelings for him?* Belle hoped not – it would only complicate things when it was time for him to leave.

She backed away then. "It must be nearly time to open the store." Before he could respond she hurried to the store and turned over the open sign. Moments later, Mrs. Grayson arrived. Belle took a deep breath. As much as she loved the town's matchmaker and her bigger-than-life personality, she could be quite overwhelming at times.

"Good morning, Belle," Mrs. Grayson said as she tried to peer into the kitchen. "Is Mr. Bligh here yet?

What is he making today?" She stretched her neck so far, Belle was certain Mrs. Grayson would topple over.

"Good morning, Mrs. Grayson." Caleb's booming voice called back, then he appeared carrying a tray. "Taffy is the treat of the day – if you're interested." He raised his eyes and grinned. "I'm sure I'll make something else later, but this is today's offering so far."

"Ooooh, I do enjoy having you here in Dewberry, Mr. Bligh. I'm quite certain our Belle does too." The last was loaded, and they all knew it. The old lady was most likely commenting on Belle and Caleb being matched, rather than anything to do with the store. The two shared a glance, but neither said a word. What would her customer say if she found out they'd shared a kiss? More likely than not, she'd insist the two marry.

Belle sighed. It was not a distressed kind of sigh, it was the dreamy kind that you had when thinking about someone you liked far more than you should. *What would it be like being married to Caleb?* Belle shook herself mentally – that was not going to happen, so there was no point even thinking about it.

"Where would you like me to put these?" He snatched one off the top and handed it to Mrs.

Grayson. "I thought you might like a sample. We won't tell anyone else. Deal?"

"Deal," she said through the taffy already stuffed into her mouth. "Oh, this is delicious, Mr. Bligh. There must be a way to convince you to say in Dewberry. If for no other reason, but to supply the store with these delicacies."

She raised her eyebrows as she continued to chew, and Caleb shrugged his shoulders. Belle had no idea how to answer that either. Instead Belle smiled and went back to filling the glass cabinets with candies. She straightened her window display as Mrs. Grayson continued to enjoy her piece of taffy.

"Fill one of those small boxes with taffy would you, my dear?" She grinned at Belle. "That will make a wonderful gift." Belle had not long filled the festive box when more customers began to pile into the store out of the cold. "I wonder what else Mr. Bligh will make for us today," she said, glancing at the other ladies in the store.

"No idea," Mrs. Halicourt said. "But I know it will be wonderful!"

Belle heard Caleb chuckling from the kitchen. He was certainly in his element, and thoroughly enjoying himself. She envisioned him opening cupboards and pulling down ingredients and wondered what he was creating. No matter what it was, her customers would snap it up, and she would be forever grateful. Her store was now a hive of activity, and she was finally seeing a decent profit. But soon that would change.

The last of the customers had left, and the taffy completely sold out. Having a Master Candy Maker on the premises was as exciting for her customers as it was for her. That gave Belle a sudden thought, and she hurried to the kitchen to put her idea to Caleb. He was busy measuring ingredients, so she said not a word while she waited for him to finish. As he began stirring the mixture over the stove, she breached the subject. "I know you won't be here much longer, but we have the Christmas Extravaganza coming up, and I wondered…" He glanced up and frowned.

"The Christmas what?"

"Extravaganza. It's something the owners of all the shops put on each year to bring in customers." She ran her fingers across the work bench. It had been scrubbed again. Caleb was meticulous about the cleanliness of the kitchen, as she was. "Every store does some sort of demonstration." She sighed. She enjoyed the sales the Christmas Extravaganza brought but hated trying to come up with a new idea every year.

"And you wondered if I would do the demonstration this year." His eyes pierced hers as he studied her.

It was obvious he was going to decline the invitation.

"I did. But I don't want you to feel obligated."

He stirred the mixture once more, then stepped toward her. "Belle," he said gently. "By Christmas, I'll be long gone."

Her heart thudded. He was right, and she knew it. Why she even broached the subject she didn't know. Perhaps it was wishful thinking. He took both her hands in his and brought one to his lips. "I wish I could say otherwise, but once this blizzard, if it ever happens, has been and gone, I will be too." He dropped her hands and went to stir the candy mixture again.

Her eyes stung, and she fought back tears. Her heart was breaking at the thought he wouldn't be there anymore, but she refused to cry in front of him. Knowing the sort of person Caleb was, he would take her in his arms and comfort her. It was the last thing Belle wanted because it would make her yearn for him even more. Instead she nodded to his back, and returned to her little store, wiping at her cheeks, and feeling grateful he was facing the other way.

Chapter Eight

Caleb stared down into the large pot. If it wasn't for this peppermint candy cane mixture being so far along, he'd abandon it right now. All he wanted to do was hold Belle in his arms and never let her go. He'd studied her for days now, and it was clear she was not interested in him, or any other man for that matter. He'd heard determined spinsters were like that, and she seemed to confirm it. His head pounded. Not because he was unwell, but because he was heartbroken.

When he held her in his arms, he was in heaven. When he kissed her, it was pure bliss, and he felt like he was floating on air. He'd already stayed too long in Dewberry. Heck, he wished he'd never come here. That way he would never have met her.

Deep in his heart, Caleb knew it wasn't true. He'd been here little more than a week and had fallen in love with the candy store owner. His soulmate. The woman he was meant to spend the rest of his life with.

If he had to leave, it had to be soon. Otherwise he would be far too entrenched in this little town and it's weird and wonderful citizens. As much as Mrs. Grayson irritated him by trying to match the two of them up, she was a kind lady, and he'd come to see her as a grandmother figure. If he thought it would help, he'd talk to her, but knew it would only encourage the town matchmaker. She would be in her glee as his heart slowly broke.

He poured the mixture into one of the flat pans, then added red coloring to the portion still in the pot, and stirred it vigorously, finally pouring it into the other flat pan. Now to let it set. He was really enjoying making candy again – he hadn't realized how much he missed it until now. Caleb knew he could happily stay here and make candy for the rest of his life, especially if it meant he was able to spend his days with Belle.

His heart thudded. He had a whole different life away from Dewberry, and until now, he'd enjoyed that life. But things had changed, and he would never be the same again, would never enjoy traveling again. Not unless Belle was with him. And for that to happen, she had to become Belle Bligh.

These revelations nearly knocked him off his feet. Caleb didn't know what had come over him. Was it divine intervention? Was God telling him that fate had stepped in? That God had stepped in and shown him the true direction his life should be taking?

Caleb closed his eyes and bowed his head. He silently prayed for the answers he needed, to be shown the way. When he opened his eyes again, Caleb knew what he had to do – he'd been touched by the hand of God, and nothing would ever be the same again.

Belle stared out the window. There was an eerie silence, and she knew it was time. The blizzard was coming, and soon.

She went to the door and glanced about. Not a soul was in sight, and the snow was heavier than before. She was tempted to lock the door, but left it open as it might turn out to be the last place of refuge for some poor soul who found themselves caught in the storm. Snow was piled up against the door, and it was hard to open, but she pushed it until it moved. It could mean the difference between life and death for someone, and Belle had no intention being the reason someone lost their life.

Once cleared, she hurried to the kitchen. Caleb glanced up from what he was doing. Worry shrouded his face as he studied her. "What's wrong?" he asked urgently, then hurried toward her, his arms surrounding her.

"The blizzard is about to hit."

They walked to the entrance, and he stared out of the closed door. "It seems calm, but is more than a little unnerving."

She nodded, then guided him back to the large kitchen. "We're safer in here, away from the window and door. I do hope Mrs. Grayson and the others all got home safely."

He reached out and squeezed her hand. "I hope so too." Belle knew there was nothing they could do if they weren't tucked safely inside – it was far too late for that. She watched as Caleb calmly finished making his peppermint candy canes.

"I need to do this, or they'll set hard and it will be too late." She raised her eyebrows. Well, she did say they were safe in the kitchen.

Once done, he added some logs to the fire, then began pulling ingredients down from the cupboard. "You're making more candy? What about the blizzard?"

He grinned. "You did say it was safe in here, and there's nothing else to do." He shrugged his shoulders then, and she realized his mere presence was making her feel safer, and helping to keep her calm. When she thought about it, Belle realized her heart rate had slowed down. When she understood the blizzard was on its way, her heart had pounded, and panic had set it.

As though he knew she was in a state of near panic, his arms enveloped her, and she felt comforted. Without warning, there was a loud bang and the sound of broken glass. "Stay here," he said, then ducked out to the store. He returned in record time. "The glass from the door is broken, but the window still appears to be intact. I'm going to bring the candies from the window display in here – just in case."

He began to return to the store, and Belle followed him. "Go back to the kitchen," he said. "I want you to be safe."

"We can clear it in half the time with the both of us working," she said, beginning to remove the trays from the window." Caleb nodded, undoubtedly knowing she was right. As she glanced out the window again, Belle couldn't see beyond the store. The blizzard had well and truly arrived.

The kitchen work bench was now covered. They decided to remove everything in the store, including the candies in the glass cabinet. The last thing either of them wanted to see was wasted candies due to shattered glass.

The noise of the blizzard was loud, and Belle was glad Caleb was forced to stay. Who knows where he might have been when the blizzard hit otherwise.

Although he might have already arrived at his next destination. Either way, she was glad he was here with her.

An almighty explosion had her jumping into Caleb's arms. It sounded as though the main window was shattered, and she was extremely grateful for his foresight to remove the products there. Her heart pounded, and she was breathing heavily at the fright she'd just had. Again she was grateful for his presence, and for his comforting arms. She leaned her head against his chest and heard his heart racing, much like hers. On the outside he didn't seem concerned, but he'd kept himself grounded for her, Belle was certain of it.

They stood there for what seemed the longest time, not saying or doing anything. All she wanted right now was to be in Caleb's arms, and never to leave them. When the noise subsided, she glanced up into his face. His eyes met hers, and he suddenly leaned into her, and kissed her lips, bringing a hand up to caress her cheek.

He pulled back and she rested her head once again. "I have fallen in love with you, Belle Armstrong," he said quietly, and she gasped. Belle glanced up at him again.

"I, I didn't know," she said quietly. "I didn't know what I would do once you left. I feel the same way."

He leaned back and cupped her face with both his hands, then leaned in and kissed her thoroughly. "I guess there's nothing else for it – we'll just have to get married."

Belle's eyes opened wide in anticipation. Did he say what she thought he'd said? "Are you asking me…"

"I certainly am." He suddenly dropped to one knee. "Belle Armstrong," he said, reaching for a peppermint candy cane. "Will you marry me?"

She glanced at the candy cane held in his hand. *What was he doing?* "Yes, I will!" she said, right before he hooked the candy cane over her ring finger. Belle couldn't help but laugh.

And then he kissed her more thoroughly than he had ever done before.

It was some hours later when Belle awoke in a daze. She lay on the floor, under the work bench in the kitchen – in Caleb's arms. She stared into his face – he really was a handsome man. And he was *her* man. At least he was if he meant what he'd said earlier. That he wanted to marry her.

Or perhaps it was the stress of the blizzard talking.

Belle knew that wasn't true. The Caleb she'd come to know would never play a trick like that, intentional or otherwise. He was not a prankster, and was the furthest thing from a liar you could get. It wasn't a figment of her imagination either. Caleb had asked her to marry him, and she still had the candy cane *ring* in her hand to prove it.

That thought made her giggle. She tried to stifle it so she didn't wake him. The more she tried, the harder it became, and the more insistent the giggle became, until she was visibly shaking. Finally the sound came out of her mouth, and she couldn't stop it.

Caleb opened his eyes, seemingly as disoriented as she was when she first awoke. It must be late evening because the room was in semi-darkness, embers from the fire their main source of light. He seemed to get his bearings, then stared into her face.

"What's so funny?" He straightened his legs. They were probably numb, as hers were. On the cold floor underneath the large work bench was not the most comfortable place to be, but he thought it might be the safest until the storm passed, and Belle agreed. So they'd crawled there after removing everything from the store, and held each other tight. Well, Caleb held her tight. He'd vowed to protect her, and that's exactly what he did.

She held out the hand that still cradled the candy cane, and he smiled. The thought of that moment sent warmth soaring through her despite the cold floor they lay on. He leaned in and kissed her gently.

The bell on the shattered front door tinkled. "Oh my." Of all people, it was Mrs. Grayson. Before either of them had a chance to remove themselves from under the table, the determined matchmaker was in the kitchen, bending down to stare at them both. Her eyes pierced Caleb's.

Belle clambered up and Caleb followed. "It's all right," Belle told her, holding up her candy cane clad hand. "We're engaged."

The giggle that had overtaken her earlier came unbidden this time, and Caleb joined in. A huge grin crossed the matchmaker's face, and she stepped forward to hug them both.

Epilogue

Two years later…

"Can everyone see?" Caleb glanced about the work bench that was now surrounded by curious onlookers. "Good, we'll get started then."

Mrs. Grayson was right at the front. She would not let an opportunity pass her by to be at the center of attention, and Caleb knew it. "What are you making?" There was a twinkle in the old lady's eye. She knew exactly what he was making because she'd attended every one of his demonstrations, if not for any other reason but to support him.

"I'm making taffy. Provided you're not impatient, anyone can make this at home." They could, but Caleb knew they wouldn't. It was time consuming, and you needed agility to be able to pull the mixture for some time to get the right consistency. He'd already done the messy part where he had to boil the sugar and other ingredients. The demonstrations were timed to be at precisely the moment the mixture was ready for this part.

"The ingredients you need for this item are…" he went on to state the ingredients but not quantities, knowing not a single attendee would be interested in making such a large batch of taffy. As he stretched the taffy, pulling this way and that, he had to force back a grin. He was entertained by the visitor's antics as they were by what he was doing.

"Now that it is ready – you would have noticed the change in color – it's time to cut it up." He broke the mixture into six smaller batched and rolled until it was the thickness he required. Caleb reached for the dough scraper he'd bought specifically for this purpose. It made cutting candy far easier. "Next it is cut into bite sized pieces." He proceeded to cut one strip of the candy, and placed it on a small platter. "Pass that around, would you, Mrs. Grayson? You can have two for your trouble." He winked at her, and the older lady blushed.

"They'll be a little stickier than you're used to – that's because they haven't had time to set properly. They may also be a bit warm."

"Mmmmm," was all he heard for the next few minutes. Belle sat back watching, as she loved to do. One year old Jeremy sat quietly on her knee, waiting for the moment when his father had finished the demonstration.

The moment he climbed down and ran toward his father, Belle's swollen belly was clear for all to see.

Almost the moment the ladies finished their piece of taffy, Buck Holman entered the kitchen. "All candies are ten percent off for the next fifteen minutes," he announced, then quickly returned to the store.

Belle came across to Caleb, and he put his arm around her, pulling her close, and holding their son at the same time. "I'm glad we took a chance on young Buck. He's a wonderful apprentice, and one of these days, he might open a store of his own."

Belle's wish to become Caleb's apprentice had come true for a while, but it was difficult to make candy with little ones hanging of your skirts. And dangerous. It wasn't long before she had to stop, but vowed to get back to it one day. In the meantime, not only had Caleb found a great apprentice in Buck, but it had put a stop to the young man's destructive behavior. He'd needed someone to believe in him, and guide him in the right direction. That person was Caleb, and he couldn't be more proud of Buck, and what he'd since become.

"He deserved a second chance," Belle said quietly.

Caleb glanced down at her, then kissed her forehead. "He did indeed, and look at him now."

Candies Galore had become of one the most sought-after candy stores in the region, bringing more tourists to Dewberry Lane than ever before. Not that anyone minded, but they did want to preserve that small town feel. Luckily most of their itinerant customers came when the stagecoach arrived. A group of tourists headed straight to the candy store, spending a chunk of their precious time there, until it was time to eat and then were on their way again.

Belle reached for his hand, and placed it on her belly. A slow grin crossed his face as he felt the little human kicking her mama's belly. If this one should be a girl, they'd decided to name her Ethel, after Mrs. Grayson who'd matched the pair, although she didn't do much to get them together. Fate and chemistry took care of that.

"That's your little sister," Caleb told Jeremy, although he was far too young to understand. He would make a great big brother, looking out for his baby sister, Caleb was certain. One day, if he was interested, he too would become Caleb's apprentice. His father, the original Jeremy Bligh, had given Caleb a precious gift, one he hadn't appreciated until he came to Dewberry.

He was an extremely lucky man, he knew. The special gifts given to him were not materialistic, but precious, nonetheless. His wonderful family were his most cherish gifts of all. If he hadn't stopped at Dewberry, none of this would have happened.

He closed his eyes and silently prayed his thanks for everything God had bestowed upon him. Without His intervention, none of this would have occurred, and he would be a man bereft of the most important things in life – family and love.

The End

From the Author

Thank you so much for reading my book – I hope you enjoyed it.

I would greatly appreciate you leaving a review where you purchased, even if it is only a one-liner. It helps to have my books more visible!

About the Author

Multi-published, award-winning and bestselling author Cheryl Wright, former secretary, debt collector, account manager, writing coach, and shopping tour hostess, loves reading.

She writes both historical and contemporary western romance, as well as romantic suspense.

She lives in Melbourne, Australia, and is married with two adult children and has six grandchildren. When she's not writing, she can be found in her craft room making greeting cards.

Links:

Website: *http://www.cheryl-wright.com/*

Blog: *http://romance-authors.com/*

Facebook Reader Group:
https://www.facebook.com/groups/cherylwrightaut hor/

Join My Newsletter:

https://cheryl-wright.com/newsletter/